IN THE
MOUTH
OF THE
WOLF

MICHAEL MORPURGO
ILLUSTRATED BY BARROUX

EGMONT

We bring stories to life

First published in Great Britain 2018
by Egmont UK Limited
The Yellow Building, 1 Nicholas Road, London W11 4AN

Text copyright © 2018 Michael Morpurgo
Illustrations copyright © 2018 Barroux

ISBN 978 1 4052 8526 1

65511/1

A CIP catalogue record for this title is available from the British Library

Printed and bound in Great Britain by the CPI Group

For Nan and Francis,

Niki, Jay, Christine and Paul.

And Kia.

Michael Morpurgo

In memory of Yves Barroux.

For Marie-Thérèse and Sophie-Laure.

BARROUX

HAPPY BIRTHDAY TO ME

They gave me such a jolly party today. Everyone from the village came.

Ninety years old, I am. I'm walking a bit stooped these days, and my knees and hips are more rickety than they should be, but I can walk up into the village, and I still like a good meal, and a glass of good red wine – I had plenty of that this evening. Sleep does not come so easily as it did, but I mustn't grumble. I have my memories, and friends all around me, and family too, those who are still alive. What more could an old man want?

FRANCIS

A better memory would be good. I'm fine with faces
and places. It's the years that get muddled, jumbled up. I
spend my time trying to unjumble them.

The village mayor made a generous speech, and
said how honoured they were to have Monsieur le
Colonel Francis Cammaerts – such a great man,
and such a great friend to the people of Le Pouget,

and of France – living here in their little French village, and his family too. The school children stood in the courtyard, with their Union Jack and Tricolour flags, and sang 'Sur le Pont d'Avignon' and 'London Bridge is Falling Down' as well, and everyone clapped and sang 'Happy Birthday to You', in English and in French.

A little girl stepped forward to present me with some flowers. Red, white and almost-blue irises. Lovely. The mayor said she was the newest girl in the school, that she had recently come from Punjab to live in the village. She spoke with quiet dignity, and in good French. 'I am Jupjaapun Kaur. From all the children in Le Pouget I wish you a most happy birthday.' I repeated her name again and again to be sure I was pronouncing it right.

She smiled at me, and told me that Kaur means princess. The flowers, she said, came from her garden.

I was so glad at that moment that we'd come back to live in France, but sad that not all of us were here, that Nan and our Christine were not with us. Several others too. I miss them more today than ever. But I have Paul, and I have Niki. And Jay.

A wonderful son and two dear daughters, and little Kia, who is no longer little at all – grandchildren grow up even faster than your own children. I should be thankful.

4

And I am, I am. But I am in the dusk of my life, a dusk that is streaked with joys, and sadnesses.

I was suddenly tired and longing for the solitude and quiet of my little room, and bed. I waved them all goodbye. Jay helped me into the house, and into bed, hugged me and left. What children I have, what friends they are to me!

So here I am now, in my bed. Night has fallen. The bright moon shining in through the window, and the church bell striking midnight. My scops owl hoots his birthday greeting to me. I smile in the moonlight and settle back on my pillows. I know I won't sleep.

This is a night for remembering. I want to remember everyone who wasn't here at my party, all my good companions in life who held my hand, stroked my brow, helped me through. I want to see them again, be with them again, live all my life with them again, from my sandpit days to now. Ninety years.

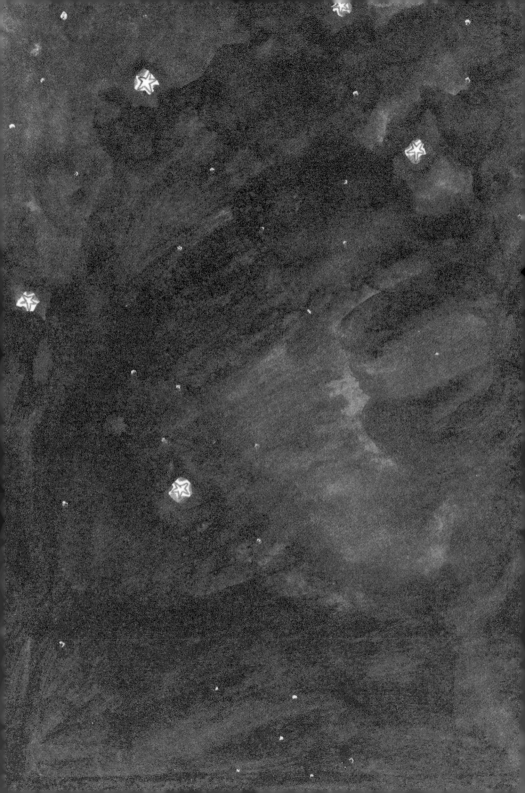

SANDPIT DAYS

Papa, are you there, Papa? You missed a good party. I think of you, and you are sitting there in your tweed suit, with your bird's nest of a beard, wreathed in pipe smoke. I always wanted to be like you, Papa, smoke a pipe, write fine poetry, stories and plays, be wise. You were so wise about most things – but not everything. For a start, you had far too many children. Four daughters, all of them loud with laughter and full of opinions – Marie, Elizabeth, Catherine, Jeanne – and then there was Pieter and me;

'the boys', you called us. There were children tumbling everywhere, crowding me out of the sandpit, and forever making plays where I always had to be a tree, because I was tall.

The sisters chose the plays, took the main parts too. Pieter was the best actor, but they made him play the log that Bottom sat on in *A Midsummer Night's Dream*.

Do you remember that, Papa? And I was a tree again of course. You said Pieter made a very fine log, but you said nothing about me being a very fine tree.

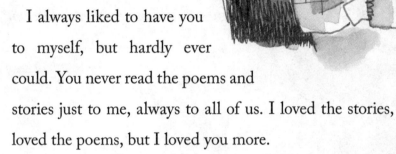

I always liked to have you to myself, but hardly ever could. You never read the poems and stories just to me, always to all of us. I loved the stories, loved the poems, but I loved you more.

You remember those summer holidays in Belgium, Papa, the country walks in the Ardennes forest where you had grown up as a child? Those were the best times, Papa, just you and me, and Pieter trailing along behind, waving a stick. He always had a stick. I asked him once why he was fencing with it, and he said he was fighting off the wolves. And I said there was no need to fight them, that he could turn and face them, and clap his

hands and look brave. And Pieter said no, that if they came close and bared their teeth, if they wanted to eat him up, if they wanted to tear our family to pieces, he had to fight them.

You said, Papa, in your wisdom, in your desire always to be fair, that we were both right. But you had told me all my life that it was ignorance and ancient hatreds and power politics that had dragged Europe into the horrors of the Great War, and that in that war, as in all wars, there were never winners, only sufferers. You set me on my pacifist course early, Papa. It is a philosophy that has guided me and troubled me all my life.

Who knows why you sent me off to that boarding school, banishing me from the family home, from all that was familiar – from you? I was never so miserable, before or since. I lay in my bed each night and raged against you and Mama. I grew away from you, from home and family, more and more each night. In time, Pieter came to join me, and we should have been allies then. But I

was older, taller, domineering, and I am ashamed to say, Papa, that I neglected him dreadfully. Worse, I turned my back on him as a brother. He was a new boy, a squirt. I treated him with disdain, disowned him sometimes. I have never forgiven myself.

If I am honest, I think there was jealousy there. I might have been a big cheese, was taller than any other boy in the school, a giant on the rugby field, always surrounded by friends, but Pieter was beautiful, with the face of a young god, kind-hearted always, Mama's favourite, and at home so full of fun and laughter. But not at school. This was not a place for sensitive souls. He hated it as much as I did.

* * *

You didn't know any of this, did you, Papa? We kept our school life separate, Pieter and I. At home I could be more like a proper brother to him again. Free from the tyranny of that school, we could be ourselves, be brothers, be the best of friends. But, away from you, Papa, I stopped

knowing you. I stopped knowing you, even stopped loving you for a while. Home was a foreign land to me. You were busy becoming Emile Cammaerts, travelling up to London every day, the great professor and poet.

There were no more family holidays in the Ardennes, no more walks and talks in the forest, just you and me. There was civil war raging in Spain, Hitler's bombs were falling on Guernica, on families, on old and young alike. And in Germany and in Italy, fascists were on the move. The world was resounding to the march of jackboots, the drums of war were beating.

I did my university degree in Cambridge, living the last of the good life, turning a blind eye, hoping for the best, but fearful already that the Great War into which I had been born was not going to be the war to end all wars. I turned to teaching, not out of conviction, not yet, but for lack of anything else to do. You approved, and told me I would make a great teacher. I wanted so much to believe that.

I hardly saw Pieter those days. He was going his own way, as a proper actor – not just a log any more – travelling the country. If I ever came home, you would show me his reviews proudly. You forgave me for drifting away, let me become whoever I was going to become. You trusted me, and that takes love, I know that now. You made me who I am, Papa. And Pieter? Well, Pieter changed the whole course of my life.

A STAR IN THE MAKING

The scops owl is still hooting to the world, to me, wishing me a happy birthday. But the church bell has chimed one o'clock. So my birthday is well and truly over. A cloud is passing over the moon, darkening my room. I don't like the dark, never have. Nor did Pieter. He hated to be alone at night. When he was little he often used to come into my room and crawl into my bed. I never told Pieter I was frightened of the dark too. We used to count the stars we could see to take our minds off the dark, and I would teach him the names of all the stars I knew. He told me once how much he longed to go there, to the stars.

* * *

You there, Pieter? You up there in the stars? Missed you at the party. Or were you there maybe? Been a long time, little brother. What is it, nearly seventy years since I watched you get on that chuffa-chuffa train, as you used to call them, at Radlett Station? I knew then, as the train pulled out and you were waving at me out of the window, that I wouldn't see you again. As you disappeared into the smoke, I wanted to shout after you to come back. I glimpsed it in your face, that you knew what I feared, that you didn't need me to warn you. You were doing what you believed was right. You didn't need me at all, not any more. What you didn't know, because I never told you, was how much I needed you then and have needed you since, every day, all my life.

* * *

We did everything together, didn't we, Pieter? With Papa away at work up in London even during the school holidays, you were the only one at home I could really talk to. We swam, we cycled, we climbed trees, we learnt to drive together, learnt about girls together too. Learning to drive was a whole lot easier.

There came a day when we had both grown away from home, and were not big brother and little brother any more. I had left university and you were at drama college and were acting at Stratford-upon-Avon – *Julius Caesar*, it was, and you were the best actor in the play, no question. I was so proud of you in your toga, so envious of your great gift. How could that little boy who had trailed behind me in the forest, fencing off the wolves with his stick, longing to go to the stars, have become such a great actor?

We took a rowing boat out for a picnic on the river, tied up under a willow tree, and we talked properly, maybe for the first time. We argued, not angrily but passionately, about Hitler and Mussolini, about the war we knew was coming. I spoke of the futility and waste of war, of the barbarity and horror of the Great War, of how we must not descend to the level of the fascists and join in another conflict that would only serve to kill more millions. I insisted that pacifism was the only way forward for humanity.

And you surprised me with the force of your argument. You said that you had always respected my views, but that I was wrong, that pacifism would not stop Hitler, that the cruelty of fascism had to be confronted. Hitler had marched into Austria, and into Czechoslovakia and Poland, and everyone knew his tanks would soon be rolling into Alsace-Lorraine, you said. The freedom of Europe, of the whole world, was threatened. If it came to war, you would join up and fight. You said you loved acting, but you couldn't go on making make-believe on the stage when the survival of everyone and everything you held dear was at stake. And I told you – and how well I remember saying it – that killing another human being,

no matter how worthy the cause, was wrong, was as wicked as any evil, as any tyrant you might be fighting. Wars solve nothing. I was adamant.

You simply smiled at me as you were rowing, and said, 'We must each do what we must do, Francis.' Then you looked down at my bare feet in the bottom of the boat, and laughed. 'Strewth, I had forgotten what big feet you have! That's what they called you at school, you know, when you weren't listening. "Big Feet".' You wriggled your own feet then, and said, 'See those? Small feet, Francis. I always wanted them to be bigger, like yours. I think maybe we all have to get used to our own feet.' This was my new brother, no longer little, a brother with a mind of his own, a wonderful man.

So you went your way, and I went mine. Neither you nor I wrote letters if we could help it. We met occasionally, awkwardly, at family gatherings which I never enjoyed. The family gloried in your success and would send me reviews from time to time. 'Pieter Cammaerts is remarkable, a tour de force.' 'Pieter Cammaerts, a star in the making.'

And whilst you were gathering these accolades during that last spring and summer of peace, I was still trying to discover where my big feet might take me. You had always been so sure of yourself. You set out to be a great actor and that's what you became. As for me, I found myself one day standing there in front of a class of forty children, trying to be a teacher. Teach and teach well, I thought, give the children the opportunities they deserve. That was the only way to make the world a better, more peaceful place.

You know me, Pieter, ever full of high-minded notions and pontifications. But these notions weren't of much use to me in front of all those children, most of whom were not at all keen to learn. Being big and tall helped, I found. I frightened them at first. 'Mr Giant' they called me. 'Big Feet' too. I would sometimes hear a whispered chorus of 'Fee fi fo fum', when they saw me coming.

I learnt plenty from one or two other teachers at the

school, Harry in particular. He taught me that you had to be on their side, and they had to know it, that mutual respect and affection was the key. I was discovering for myself that I had in the class forty expectant faces gazing up at me, forty intellects waiting to be stimulated, forty hearts waiting to be moved to laughter or tears, through stories and poems and plays. I had to get to know what made each of them tick, and to do that I had to learn to listen to them, and understand them. They had to know they had a friend in me as well as a teacher.

I tried to pass on to them all the things I had loved as a child, all I had done with you and Papa in the Ardennes. I walked the river banks with them, looking for otters and herons and kingfishers, walked the wild woods when the bluebells were out, discovered foxholes with them, watched larks rising over the fields. It was quite unexpected, but I fell in love with teaching, and knew quickly I would make it my life.

But much like you with your acting, Pieter, Adolf Hitler changed all that. He marched his armies into Poland, as you had said he would, bombed Warsaw. Still I hoped and believed there could be peace. Can you imagine? I saw what was happening, we all did. His tanks roared into Holland, through the Ardennes, through Papa's forest, our forest, into our beloved Belgium.

You did what you said you would, left your toga behind in the theatre, and put on your blue RAF uniform instead. And you looked perfect in that part too. You were training for months somewhere up in Scotland, but you didn't want to talk about it. All you said was that now you were a Sergeant Navigator you probably knew the stars better than I did.

We had a last Sunday lunch back at home with the family, you in your uniform. Then I walked you to the station and we waited for your train over a cup of tea. There was a silence between us, not because we were strangers – it was more a silence of foreboding. It was raining when the train came in. We held on to one another, neither of us wanting to let go. You went on waving from the train window for as long as you could see me. And that was that.

You went off west to join your bomber squadron in Cornwall, and I went off north to Lincolnshire, to work on a family farm. I had had to go before a tribunal to explain why I felt I would not and should not put on a uniform and fight in this war, or any war. They had listened grim-faced, told me I was wrong, but accepted my sincerity. I had to contribute to the war effort in other ways, they said. I would have to go to work on a farm. The nation needed food.

So I found myself milking cows, mucking them out, feeding pigs, mucking them out, feeding hens, mucking them out. Lots of mucking out. I loved the sheep best, especially lambing time. I drove the tractor, helped with the hay and straw harvest, dug up turnips and potatoes. I learnt more in a few months, Pieter, than I had in all my time in university. I grew fit and strong too, and that was to be important.

In the farmhouse I lived amongst fellow pacifists, all of us wanting to forget the war, but never being able to.

We read poetry, made music and plays, but when we talked, it was of the war. And the radio was there to remind us all the time of the real world outside. Defeat was in the air. There was Dunkirk, the threat of imminent invasion, the Blitz on London, on Coventry, on cities all over the country. Everywhere it seemed Hitler was triumphant: in France, in Norway, in Africa. And still I convinced myself that the world would see sense, that somehow a peace could be made, that I had been right all along.

I happened to be back at Papa and Mama's house in Radlett, on one of my rare visits – I can't remember why. The phone rang at breakfast. Papa answered. Mama and I went on talking for a while, then realised he was saying nothing, and saw his shoulders crumple as he listened. He put the phone down, and turned to face us. We knew before he said the words. 'Pieter is dead. That was his Commanding Officer from his squadron in Cornwall. His plane crashed.'

They told us later you were on an air raid over occupied France, and the plane had been hit by anti-aircraft fire. The pilot was badly wounded so you tried to fly the plane home over the Channel. You made it to the Cornish Coast, told the rest of the crew to jump, and then tried to land. But you were a Sergeant Navigator, not a pilot. You had never flown a plane before. You crashed. The pilot died. You died.

I did not know it at the time, Pieter, but that phone call, your dying so young, at twenty-one, set me on a new course in my life. By your death you won the argument. Somehow I had to find a way to set my pacifism to one side and join the struggle, join the fight against those who had killed you.

You reached for the stars, Pieter. I can see the Plough from my window. You always loved the Plough best. You are up there somewhere, Pieter, ploughing a new furrow, looking down on me from time to time, looking after me. You have always been looking after me, ever since.

EAT NO MORE CABBAGE

That wretched church bell has kept me awake, tossing and turning through many more nights than I care to remember. But tonight I need that bell. I have to stay awake and I feel sleep coming over me. I want them all here with me, not to celebrate – the celebration is over, all the eating and drinking, and talk and laughter, all the speeches and singing – but to remember, even if it is sometimes painful. I have lived through long years of joy and pain, maybe in equal measure. I must remember as clearly as I can, never avoiding difficulty and sadness and regret. Nan always stopped me wallowing in that, said it did no one any good, that what was done, was done. Always the pragmatist, my Nancy was. It's been so hard to go on without her.

* * *

Nan? I hope you are listening. Sometimes I think I talk to you more now than I ever did when you were there to talk to.

Oh, what you did for me, Nan! You stayed, put up with me, saw us through the bad times and the good. You let me gallop away, leap fences, reined me in when I needed it, fed me, watered me, kept my stable bright and beautiful, whispered in my ear, forgave me for bad behaviour – of which there was plenty – ticked me off, but never shouted, brushed me down, spruced me up, cared for me, kept us together. And you put up with my silences. Not another soul would have done the same.

But I wasn't always silent, if you remember. I wasn't silent the first time you saw me, was I? I was in the tin bath in front of the stove in the farmhouse. I'd been mucking out the pigs. I was washing off the smell of

them, singing at the top of my voice to let everyone know I was in the bath, and not to walk in. I was lying back, as far as you could in those old tin baths, legs and feet hanging out over the edge, and in you came, no knocking, you just burst in.

'I'm in the bath!' I yelled.

'I can see that,' you said in your Scottish voice. Then you saw my feet. 'I know who you are,' you said. 'You're that tall fellow everyone round here is talking about. "Big Feet" they call you. They were right.' And you pealed with laughter. 'And I'm Nancy,' you said, 'Nan to my friends.'

That was it. Sitting there in the bath I thought to myself: this is the one I want to be with, to have children with, to wake up beside. You threw me a towel, and I got up out of the bath, covering myself as best I could, you putting your hands over your eyes and peeking out through your fingers.

'How did you get that tall?' you asked.

'Cabbage,' I replied.

'Well, eat no more cabbage,' you said, and you walked out laughing. I loved that laugh, loved you.

I was over the moon when I first learnt you had come to stay for a while. You were family to the Broadbents, the farming family and fellow pacifists who had become such good friends by now. We all sat around the lamp-lit table in the kitchen that evening, basking in communal friendship. After supper, you and me, Nan, we sat by the stove and talked long into the night.

And was it days or weeks? Did you ask me, did I ask you? Doesn't matter. I can't remember. Just a month or two afterwards and we were married – in secret, for which Mama never forgave us. I am so glad you got to meet Pieter, that he could be best man at our wedding.

And he was the best of men too. Soon enough there was a baby on the way. How wonderful that was in those times. In the midst of so much death and destruction, so much sadness, we were making new life. Where there was new life there would be new hope.

Yet the war would not leave us alone. Families and homes and towns were being destroyed everywhere, Hitler was marching into Russia, his armies ever victorious. The Japanese had bombed Pearl Harbour. The whole world was now at war. Lose, and the enemy would come across the Channel, occupy our villages and cities, as they had in France, and Belgium, as they had everywhere, taking what they wanted, burning what they did not. They would build their concentration camps here in Lincolnshire, in Hertfordshire, wherever they felt like it.

Around our kitchen table at supper we railed against tyranny. We talked of the struggle for freedom and rights, but still we clung to our belief that to end the life of another human being was wrong, that we should fight only with words, with education, never with hate in our hearts. But I spoke up less and less in these heated discussions. And you knew why, Nan.

Ever since the death of Pieter I had been at war with myself, pulled one way, then the other. To fight or not

46

to fight. Then the bomb fell on a farm nearby, and killed the Crosby family – all of them kind, good country people, who helped us with the harvest, who had helped mend our tractor. Some German bomber on his way home had dropped his bombs, maybe because it was safer to fly home without them. Maybe it was not intentional. But the result was the same. One coffin was so small. I saw old Mr Crosby, the grandfather, bearing it into church, behind three other coffins. All his family gone. He was not crying but staring straight ahead. He was not carrying the coffin, he was cradling it.

A few days later, you gave birth to little Niki, and I found myself walking her up and down the bedroom in my arms, cradling her, humming to her, trying to settle her. You were asleep, exhausted. She looked up into my eyes. I felt her fingers close around my thumb and hold me. Between them – Pieter, little Bessie Crosby in her coffin, and Niki cradled in my arms – they left me no choice. I would have to join up, have to play my part in the struggle. I could no longer let others do my fighting and dying for me.

I expected to have to persuade you that I was doing the right thing, but when I told you I had made up my mind to join up, you simply said, 'You must go and do what you must do, Francis. Just don't expect me to like it. And don't get yourself killed, you hear? Whatever happens, when it's over and the war is won, Niki and I will be waiting for you, and then we can pick up where we left off, can't we?'

The day after I had finally made up my mind, Harry came to visit, quite out of the blue. You remember him, Nan? My mentor, teacher and good friend from the school where I had been teaching, a kindred spirit and a fellow pacifist. We went for a long walk on the farm. I told him that I had decided I had to join up, that I was not abandoning my pacifism, but setting it to one side for a while, out of necessity. I told him I still hated the idea of killing. I wanted to find a way to fight my own war, the way I wanted to, where I knew it could make a difference.

Harry did not say much as he listened to me rambling on. Then, looking at me hard, he asked me one question. 'You speak French, don't you, Francis?' And he answered for me. 'With a rather Belgian sort of an accent, as I remember it, but that's all right. All I can do, Francis,' he went on, 'is put you in touch with a friend of mine in London. I think he might be able help you

49

find what you are looking for. I can tell you it could make a difference, could help the war effort greatly. One thing, Francis. You should say nothing to anyone about our conversation today.'

✱ ✱ ✱

When I told you that same evening, Nan, that I might have to go away soon to London, to join up, you knew better than to ask any whys or wherefores. I could say nothing and you didn't ask. So the long silence between us began, Nan, a silence that lasted on and off right through the war. I think we spent the rest of our lives afterwards healing that silence, didn't we? And you did most of the healing work. That was your great talent, Nan: reconciliation, kindness. I never in my whole life knew anyone kinder.

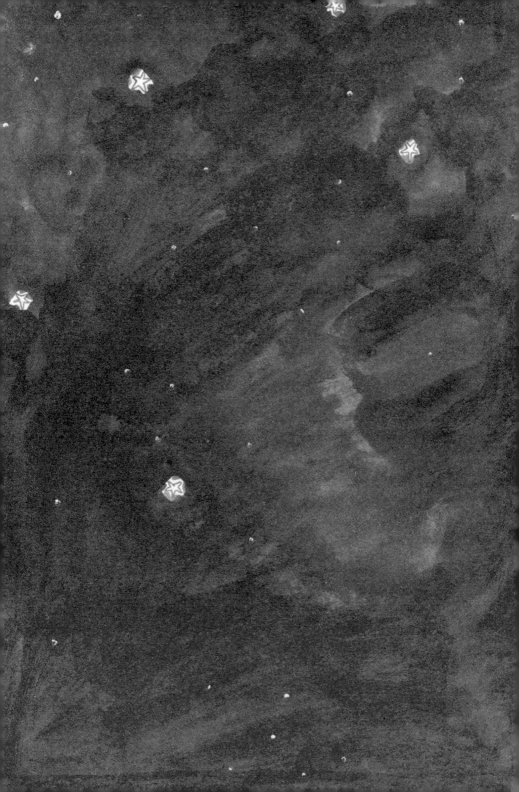

MUD AND MADNESS

Three o'clock. That church bell is cracked. It does not ring, it clangs. Soon after we moved to the village fifteen years ago I told the priest that it ought to be repaired. He told me why it should stay as it is – that the church had been damaged in the war, when a tank shell hit the tower, bringing the bell crashing down. They had no money to repair it, only to rebuild the tower and hang the bell up again, cracked as it was. The bell should serve as a reminder to us, he said, of how life goes on, of how grateful we should all be to have peace. Being new to the village then I did not argue with him. In fact, I agreed with him. But there are times in the middle of the night, like right now, when I really do not need reminding.

When I was teaching at that school with Harry, he was always persuading me to take part in out-of-school activities of all kinds: plays, rock-climbing, choir, sailing and bell-ringing. He said this was the way you got to know the children best, not in the classroom. He was right too. Harry loved bell-ringing. I didn't, but I did like the sound of six church bells pealing when we got it right. Here, in Le Pouget, there is just the one bell, and it clangs.

Did you hear those children singing at the party, Harry? Wasn't that wonderful? Takes you back, I should think, to our teaching days. Takes me back for sure. I'm not blaming you exactly, but it's your fault, Harry, that I am lying here, aged ninety and creaky in my bones, in my bed in a little village in deepest France listening to that ruddy bell. After all, you were the one who persuaded me to go up to London to meet your mysterious friend, weren't you?

I was to go to see a Mr Jepson for an interview in a hotel, near Portman Square, I think it was. I still didn't know what I was being interviewed for.

It turned out to be more of a conversation than an interview. Mr Jepson confirmed that I came highly recommended – by you, no doubt, Harry – that it was good I could speak French quite well, but on the other hand my height was a disadvantage. I looked fit and strong, which would be important – he did not say for what. We discussed my pacifism and my change of heart, which he said he found both strange and most interesting. He was probing, I felt, to discover my motivation. So I told him.

Anything I could do to see Belgium and France and the world free from the tyranny of the Nazis I would do.

He looked at me over his glasses, considering me, assessing me, before telling me that if selected there would be months of tough training ahead of me, that I must tell no one about this meeting, not even my family; that it was secret work. That was all he would say, except that he thought I was the right sort, and that I would do. After just forty-five minutes it was over. I walked out on to the street no longer a teacher or a farmer but an army officer – Second Lieutenant Francis Cammaerts.

I'll be honest with you, Harry, there were times during my training when I cursed you out loud for getting me into whatever it was I was training for. I seemed to spend most of my time crawling through mud or undergrowth,

in all weathers, climbing ropes on endless assault courses, slogging up hill and down dale, fording rushing rivers, living in draughty manor houses with perhaps a dozen others, under observation all the time, and all of us still in the dark about what this was all for.

Anyway I passed the first course somehow, and off I was sent to the next one – no chance to get home to see Nan and Niki, except for the briefest of visits. It was one course after another, endless tramping through wilderness, up on the moors of Scotland this time. They made us carry logs around – I mean massive, heavy, back-breaking logs. And then an hour or two later we would be learning to forge signatures, how to get a letter out of an envelope without opening it, and put it back in again afterwards, leaving no trace of what we had done.

We learnt about radios and codes – I was always good at that, far better than on the assault course – and map reading was important, memorising maps in our heads so we could get about the countryside, without map or compass, by day or night.

We learnt unarmed combat, a kind of jiu-jitsu or karate. We learnt to strip down weapons of all kinds – Sten guns, Bren guns – blindfolded, and then reassemble them. Then there were lots of noisy explosives, grenades, booby traps, and the like. There were endless lessons in uniform recognition: German military, SS, French police. The training was thorough and exhausting. And then they would wake me up at night sometimes, and drag me downstairs into a darkened room, shine a bright light on my face and interrogate me. I knew it was a game of course – they were not very convincing interrogators, I thought. I learnt to play the game, to stick to my prepared story, no matter what.

Of course I guessed by now what kind of war I would be involved in, that all the training and war games meant that sooner or later I might find myself in German occupied territory. I think we all knew it, but did not speak of it. Secrecy was everything. Silence was everything. You know how it was, Harry. You did the same training somewhere else, didn't you? But you never spoke of it. Not a word.

* * *

Did you have that moment, Harry, when at last all the training was over and done, and they told you what it had all been for, where they were going to send you? Did you ever look at yourself in the shaving mirror, as I did, Harry, and whisper it? 'You're a secret agent. *A secret agent.* How can you be doing this – you, a pacifist? How can this be right? I know how to kill a man, with a knife, with a pistol, with my bare hands. Will I do it? Should I?' Doubts lingered, despite Pieter, despite the decision I had made.

You met my brother Pieter, didn't you, Harry, once or twice? He was an actor, you remember, and a fine actor too? You came with me to see him once at Stratford. As I looked into that mirror, I knew it was just how Pieter must have felt before he went on stage for the first night of a play. He was playing a part. It was his job. Now it was my job. I would do it as I had seen him do it. I would not act. I would live the part, become the part, become a secret agent and leave the rest of me behind – son, brother, husband, father, pacifist, teacher – leave it all behind.

The worst thing was that I hardly ever saw Nan. We phoned, we spoke. But none of that could make the separation any easier. I was living in a different world now, a secret world. It was a cruel silence, Harry, for both of us. I could not even say goodbye to her, not properly. It was easier in a way to say goodbye to Niki. A hug was enough, a silent hug that meant everything.

Then I was gone, down to the airfield at Tangmere in West Sussex, for a final check, a last walk on English soil out to the plane waiting for me in the dark, then I was climbing up into a smelly Lysander and off to France. I thought of you as I was sitting in that plane, Harry, because I knew that somewhere you were probably doing much the same thing. And I vowed to myself then, that after it was all over, I would go back to teaching, as I knew you would too. Meanwhile down there below me in

the darkness there was an enemy to be defeated. A clever enemy, a vicious enemy.

I was flown into occupied France. They landed me, rather bumpily as I recall, in a field somewhere near Compiègne. With the engines left running, they bundled me out of the aircraft and into the sudden cold of a March night, welcoming lights and voices all around me. There was much hurried backslapping and handshaking, everyone calling me Roger. My new name, my only name now. As I was being dropped off, two other agents were being picked up by the Lysander. One called out to me as he passed: 'Good luck, and make sure you have a newspaper with you at all times. Lavatory paper's rather scarce in France these days!' Strange the things you remember.

Then the plane took off, back home, back to Nan and Niki. Looking up at the moon, I sent my love to them both, then walked away with my welcoming group, Roger now. I had in mind only one thing: my mission, to travel down to the south east and help supply the resistance fighters, to provide them with the weapons they needed, and to work with them to prepare for the landings that would be taking place on the south coast.

I knew I was in trouble right from the start. There was a curfew at night in occupied France, and here I was in a car full of men from the French Resistance being driven to Paris. They took my revolver and chucked it into a river, in case they were stopped, they said. Around every corner I expected to see a German roadblock. I tell you, Harry, I had visions of being picked up and shot within twenty-four hours of landing. Madness. Somehow we slipped through.

It did not get much better. They had a flat for me in Paris belonging to a Monsieur Marzac who, like the others in the car, was kind, hospitable, and brimming with confidence – overconfidence, I thought. The flat felt like a trap. So I spent all the next day out of it, just walking the streets of occupied Paris, browsing the bookshops, sitting in cafés, reading newspapers, and getting used to seeing German soldiers strolling through the parks.

For me, Harry, that was the biggest shock, seeing them there, owning the place, enjoying it, occupying it. Now I knew I was doing the right thing. I was supposed to meet Monsieur Marzac back at the flàt, or failing that in a café nearby. He never came to either. I knew something had gone wrong, and decided to get out of Paris and get out fast. I was on my own now. I walked to the Gare de Lyon and caught the next train down south.

I had my story ready, as I had been trained. Keep it simple, as close as possible to a truth you are familiar with. You know the routine, Harry. I was a teacher visiting family down south, recovering from jaundice – I had had jaundice, knew all about it. I had to use my story too, when questioned by a French policeman at the station. It worked! I felt a sense of such elation as I sat down on that train. I felt like a child who had told a lie to a teacher and got away with it.

I knew the village to go to down south – the name escapes me just now – where I was to meet up with fellow agents and the Resistance, where there was a safe house. Supposedly. It was a relief to find myself again amongst trusted friends I'd met in training. Auguste Floiras, the radio operator – the bravest of the brave he was. The news from Paris was as bad as it could be.

Marzac had been captured along with dozens of others. He was in the hands of the Gestapo. The entire group must have been infiltrated. Someone had talked, or there was a double agent at work.

Then a day or so later came a letter from Marzac in prison, introducing us to a German officer who was asking to be flown to London for 'talks'. It was such an obvious trick, and they believed it! After all these years I still cannot understand why they believed it. I told them we had to leave, that the safe house we were in must be compromised, must be being watched, that the Gestapo might swoop at any time. No one listened. I left. Within days the Gestapo had rounded them all up. Some ended up in concentration camps, some were shot.

It looked hopeless. All but one of my contacts had been taken prisoner. Only Auguste Floiras – Albert to all of us then – was still at liberty. He was the radio operator for the Resistance group, and as I was to discover, the best radio operator in the world. He had joined the Resistance

movement right from the moment the Germans invaded France. He looked and sounded like the French peasant farmer that he was. And he soon had good reason to loathe the Nazis. Both his wife and daughter had been taken in, and sent to a concentration camp. Without Auguste I should have been lost entirely. He knew people, people he could really trust. And, as I knew now only too well, trust was everything.

You should have met Auguste, Harry. A great and humble man, clever and fearless too. To be a radio operator, as you know, was the most dangerous job in the Resistance.

They were very often caught, and when they were, they were shot. Not Auguste. He was cleverer than the Germans, out-thought them, outfoxed them. You got me into the job, Harry. Auguste taught me how to do it, to keep ahead of the game, and stay alive. Both of you are dear friends, old comrades, brothers.

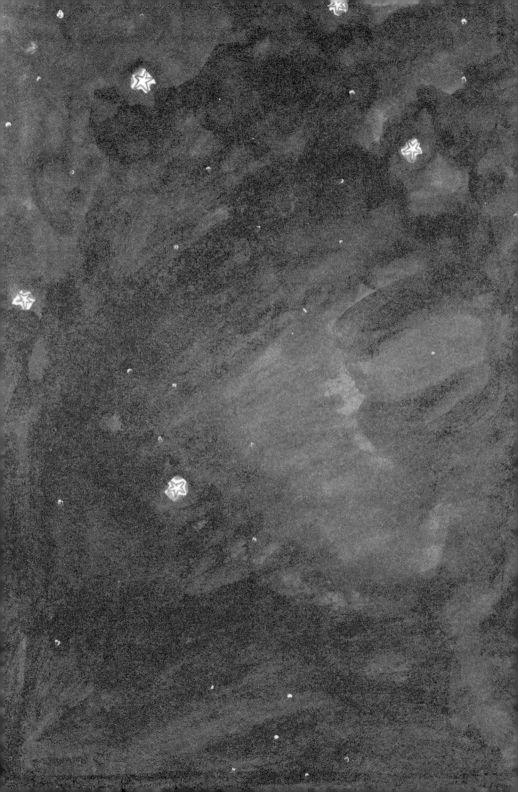

ROGER, TERRORISTE. 2,000,000 FRANCS

We made contacts wherever we could, with Auguste's friends. Stayed in barns and sheds, in mountain huts, and slept out in the open under hedges when we had to. But sometimes we found ourselves in a village like this one, in a house like this one, in a room like this one. I would peek through the shutters down into the street and see German soldiers patrolling, or the dreaded Milice, the French Nazi police. They were the worst of the worst, the most despised and the most dangerous, Auguste told me, French people who had joined the occupier, and betrayed their own. They were local, knew everyone, knew the lie of the land, had eyes everywhere.

Auguste taught me right from the start that if you wanted to stay safe you had to keep on the move, never stay in the same place for more than a couple of nights.

This was even more important, he told me, for those who were hiding us. If we were discovered, so were they. The penalty for harbouring us would be death by firing squad.

Auguste and I created, from his friends and their friends, small isolated bands of Resistance fighters, cells of no more than three or four. They knew only each other, so if captured and tortured could only betray those in their group. No group ever knew what another one was planning. Only we did, Auguste and me. No names except code names were ever used. So to everyone else we were always Roger and Albert, and no one knew who we really were, or where we were.

We became, in a few months, a small army of thousands of brothers and sisters, most unknown to one another. Nothing was ever written down unless it was to be destroyed at once. Mistakes were made, people got careless, and that cost lives. But through all the triumphs and disasters, Auguste was at my side looking out for me, for all of us.

Ninety years old. Without Auguste I would never have reached thirty.

There's that owl again, hooting away outside my window. Auguste knew his birds, their calls and cries, their haunts and habits. Pigeons were his favourite. They were best for sending messages – far safer than carrying a radio around. But the trouble was, he said, they didn't fly fast enough.

* * *

Auguste, you hear that owl? Scops owl, am I right? Not like the too-wit-too-woo of tawny owls, or the screech of barn owls. This is a French owl, hooting in French. You always knew your birds better than me. You grew up a country boy, a farm boy. You read the countryside like a familiar book, knew instinctively how to move unseen, alert in every fibre to danger. You were a creature of forest and field. All I had to do when I was with you was follow, and I knew I would be safe.

You know how I always see you, Auguste? You are sitting by a bedroom window just like this one, headphones on, your little wireless in its open attaché case on the table in front of you, and you are tapping out a message, twiddling your knobs, listening, writing with your stubby pencil. And those messages to London, to Algiers, arranging drop sites and times, brought us the weapons, the ammunition, the money, the supplies we needed to resist, to fight on.

But it was never enough, no matter how often we sent messages telling them we needed more. I just don't think they ever really understood how many fighters we had to keep supplied up in the hills. Ten thousand or more towards the end, wasn't it? They needed food, clothes, tents, blankets. You were there, you sent the messages,

Auguste, so you know. And every time you sent a message you risked your life. The Germans were out there, close by, listening for you, closing in on you.

It still angers me. But you always said that they had other things on their mind, like the liberation of Europe, the landings that everyone was longing for in France. You were always so reasonable, Auguste, so calm. And I was so angry.

＊ ＊ ＊

My job, your job, was to disrupt and destroy the enemy,
to kill, to frustrate, to inconvenience.

We blew up bridges and railway lines, a turntable in a
station yard, knocked out communications wherever we
could, and power stations like that hydroelectric plant on
the Durance, remember?

We blocked roads with fallen trees or rocks, poured sand into petrol tanks, ambushed German lorries and patrols. But the reprisals were terrible. They exterminated entire villages, out of revenge, out of hate. Remember Oradour-sur-Glane? What was it, Auguste – 642 dead, burnt alive, slaughtered? They would execute ten civilians for every German soldier we killed. But the more of us they killed, the more we knew we had to get rid of them. The more we longed for our freedom, the more determined we were to fight for it. And no one was more fiercely determined than you. These people were in your country, they were callous and brutal occupiers and you were going to drive them out. You led from the front, and we followed.

I often lie here wondering whether in the end it was worth it, Auguste, all those lives not lived, all the grieving. I know what you would say, because I remember you saying it. 'To win, to free France, we have to be as ruthless as they are, and more cunning with it.' And we were cunning too. We kept one step ahead of them.

The Gestapo knew who you were, knew who I was too. There was a price on your head, and a price on mine: two million francs each. I saw a poster of myself once. Not a good likeness. Ugly-looking fellow! 'Roger, Terroriste. 2,000,000 francs'. And in two years no one ever betrayed either of us. You told me once that with money like that, you could sell yourself and buy enough wine to keep your village happy for a lifetime!

And strewth, did we walk, Auguste! Thousands of kilometres. From group to group we went, the two of us together, organising, encouraging, promising this and that – weapons, ammunition, food, money – you tapping out my messages to London, arranging more drops to the Resistance wherever they were needed, planning more operations, and all the while training more fighters.

We used the roads as little as possible. Cross-country was best, to avoid road checks and German soldiers on the move. Skirting the villages was always safer, climbing hills, fording rivers, scrambling up and down mountains. I was forever stumbling along to keep up with you. We sang to keep up our spirits, do you remember? I taught you English songs, you taught me French ones.

I never told you, Auguste, but you sang horribly out of tune.

We went on bicycles sometimes, when we had to. We covered the distances a lot quicker that way, but it was risky. The Germans who stopped us at the road checks often weren't so bad, mostly old soldiers serving their time, wanting a quiet life. But we avoided the Milice whenever we could.

I would never have got away with it without you. You looked every inch a French peasant on your way to the next village. I always felt like a lanky Englishman, a teacher from the suburbs of London. But I must have lived my part well enough, looked thoroughly unconcerned and bored when they searched me, had a convincing story to tell, and my forged papers were always in order. I owe my life over and over again to whoever had forged those papers back in London.

And you taught me that trick of yours, Auguste. You remember? It never failed. Bite your lip when you see them, make it bleed a little. Then cough a bit as you approach, and more as you show them your papers. They see the blood on your lips. Tuberculosis. Infectious. It worked, time and again. They'd wave me through in a hurry. I learnt to freeze inside, just went numb when I was being questioned and searched. I used hate to help banish fear. That was your idea too. A bit of blood on your lip, and controlled hate in your heart.

I was never brave, Auguste, as you always said I was, as others have supposed. I simply knew I had to train myself not to feel fear, or it would show and I would give myself away. I was never brave like those farming families who looked after us, who fed us and sheltered us. They knew what would happen to them if they were caught. I think of them often – I still know a few of them.

I don't have to tell you, Auguste, after what happened

to your poor wife and daughter, but it was the women who were the bravest of the brave: the grandmothers, mothers, the aunties, the daughters. They were with us up in the mountains, waiting for the first sound of the plane coming in to make a drop in the moonlight, longing like us to hear it coming, see it coming, hearts full of hope and excitement as the parachutes opened. That was dangerous enough and they knew it.

They were the ones who helped us open the canisters and packed the explosives and guns and ammunition on to the mules to carry everything down from the mountains.

And they were the ones who hid everything in their houses, on their farms, then transported it over the countryside to the Resistance groups, sometimes on foot, by bicycle, on horse and cart, under hay, under grapes, under skirts, in prams.

And they were the ones who brought food up to the men hiding in the forests and the mountains, all of this right under the noses of the Germans. There were no medals for these women. They are the unknown, unsung heroes. That was real courage. Without them there could have been no Resistance.

You were there when Christine first came, weren't you? Out of the blue one night she dropped into the mountains, into our lives. You taught me how to organise, how to survive, Auguste. Christine saved my life. She was no angel, but she sang like one, do you remember? And she sang in tune too, Auguste!

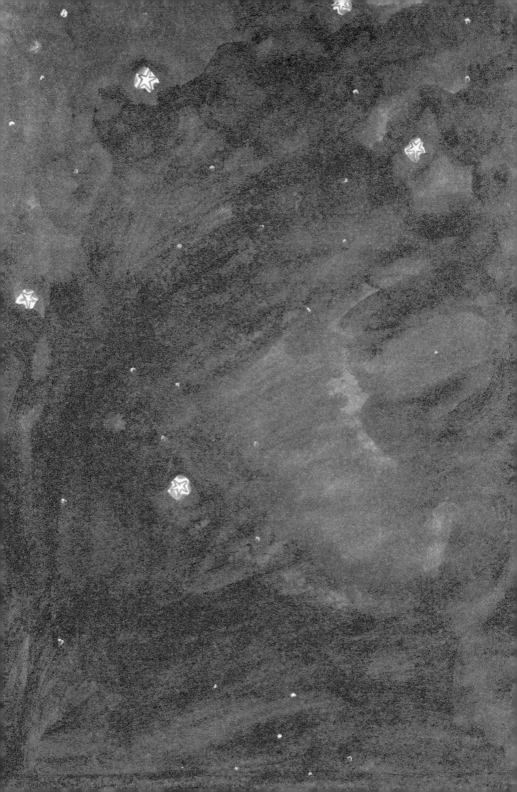

IN THE MOUTH OF THE WOLF

The nightingale is singing again – haven't heard her for a few nights. She's keeping the owl company, keeping me company. A duet! I can't sing any more. 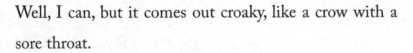 Well, I can, but it comes out croaky, like a crow with a sore throat.

I would sing often to Niki, when I came home that time from France. They flew me back to England – mostly, I think, to tick me off, because some of my messages to London had not been that polite. I had been badgering them for months to drop us more and better weapons, ammunition, more explosives, and food, but so often the canisters were dropped in the wrong place in the mountains, or the parachutes failed and they shattered on impact. At the meeting, I was angry, and gave them a piece of my mind.

I banged the table at one point. An army needs weapons and food, and above all morale, I told them. Patriotism is not enough. Courage is not enough. Starve them of what they need and they cannot and will not fight.

And another thing, I said, now that they were listening to me – I need a courier, a good one, to be my eyes and ears among this ever growing army of Resistance fighters. A woman would be best, because a woman arouses less suspicion. And she had to be the best. I needed someone I could absolutely rely on. They said they would see what they could do. I held out little hope, either for more supplies, or the courier I so badly needed. But I had said my piece, and that made me feel a lot better.

And at least now that I was home I got to see Nan and Niki. We were a family again for a few short days. To go together to the shops, to walk in the park pushing Niki in the pram, to see British soldiers and sailors in the street, and hear English spoken everywhere – it was all so strange. Another world.

I could say nothing to Nan, and she said nothing to me. We tried, but the silence was like an iceberg between us. At the end of my leave, I walked out of the house and looked back to see them both waving at me from the window. I waved back, and walked away, back into

my other life, wondering if that was the last time I would see them, whether I would ever hold the baby that I now knew Nan was expecting.

I nearly didn't get back to occupied France at all. We flew into a blizzard over the mountains, and I remember the pilot telling us it was no good, that he was turning back. Minutes later one of the engines caught fire, and we all had to jump. I landed in deep snow, knocked on the door of the first farmhouse I came to. I told them I had come from England, that I was with the Resistance. Big risk, but it was either that or freeze to death. And the good people took me in, looked after me, helped me get where I needed to go.

Lucky, lucky. I was always the lucky brother. My plane crashes and I live. Pieter's plane crashes and he dies. Pieter loved singing 'Sur Le Pont d'Avignon'. I don't know why I thought of that just now. Maybe the tune was in my head. The whole family loved that song. And so did Christine.

* * *

It's been a long time, Christine. But I don't forget. When I saw you that first time – at Saint-Martin-en-Vercors, wasn't it? – you were sitting there on the step at that little house where you were staying in the village, so at ease, friends around you, as if you had just dropped in for a visit. 'Pauline,' you said, introducing yourself, and shaking my hand. 'And I know who you are, Roger.

CHRISTINE

What they say is true – you are rather tall, like a giraffe.'

You had twisted your ankle when you parachuted in, but you never let it trouble you. You didn't let anything trouble you. You made friends so easily. Everyone who met you loved you – men, women, children, and animals too – they trusted and respected you. I was never alone in loving you. London got something right, Christine. I asked for the best and they sent me you. Albert, Roger and Pauline, 'the three musketeers' you called us.

You were already more experienced at this than any of us, had been fighting them all over Europe. As with Auguste and me, it was a personal fight. You despised the Nazis with a passion. They had occupied your beloved Poland, driven your family from their home, made a concentration camp of the country. There was nothing you would not do, would not dare, to defeat them. Your determination to overcome any difficulty, your refusal ever to be downcast, your laughter, your sense of fun – you gave us all a lift, a new energy.

You were there time and again with me up in the mountains watching the parachutes floating down in the moonlight with our supplies, every one of them, you said once, a beacon of hope. Do you remember finding those food parcels of biscuits and chocolate, and the note someone had slipped in back in England when they were packing the canisters? You read it out to us. 'Vive la France! Bravo! Give them hell!'

And you were there with me and Auguste, celebrating the highs. Like when Auguste brought me the message, by that bridge, with the two swans gliding under it – the message I had been so anxiously waiting for from London, that Nan had given birth, that we had another daughter, Jay. That all was well.

And you were there to endure and support me during the lows; the lowest of the low, when I had to execute that young man, a traitor from the Milice. I know as the officer in command I had to do it, but it felt like committing a murder, and still does all these years later. Pacifist and now executioner, uneasy and incompatible companions. But you never wavered, always reassured me that I had no choice.

And we did give them hell, didn't we, Christine? It was your idea to creep into railway yards at night and change the destination labels on the train wagons. You loved to sow confusion, make mayhem. We tore down their phone lines, ambushed them, then faded away like ghosts into the countryside. You more than anyone knew better than to fight pitched battles with them. So many in the Resistance wanted to stand and fight. You knew and I knew what would happen if we did. They had the men, the weapons, the planes, the tanks. Go in, sting them like angry wasps, you told everyone, then buzz away.

But even you could not stop our brave friends. They were all so eager to take the battle to the Germans. Too eager.

You can't blame them. They all knew that liberation was coming soon. The allies had landed in Normandy. And soon the Americans would be landing on the south coast. Freedom was there to grasp. They had lived through all these years of humiliation, seen those hated soldiers strutting through their streets, watched families and friends being taken away and executed. Their moment

had come. Had they not waited long enough?

And they all thought that the Vercors plateau, high and inaccessible in the mountains, was the perfect place to raise the French flag and make a stand. There were no Germans there. We had three thousand fighters hidden high in the forests, and the Vercors was like an impregnable fortress in the mountains, deep rock ravines all around.

I knew, you knew, Auguste knew, that we were just not well enough armed. Some of us had only old hunting rifles, and fewer than twenty rounds each. The anti-tank weapons, the guns and ammunition I had been asking and begging to be dropped for months had never come. We knew we were not ready. The Germans had tanks, fighter planes, bombers. They had gliders and parachutists. All they needed. None of this mattered now to the Resistance, nothing you nor I could say made any difference. The message had come from London: Now is the time. Rise up! So they did.

They proclaimed the free republic of the Vercors, and the Tricolour flew again proudly in every village on the plateau. Flying the flag was for us the beginning of liberation at last. Truth be told, even knowing it was an ill-advised venture, you and I were swept along in that tide of fierce pride and fervent hope.

It was Bastille Day, 14th July, and we were there in the Vercors, Christine, when those American planes came in, glittering in the morning sun. Flying Fortresses, sixty,

seventy of them, the thunder of them echoing around the mountains, a great drumroll of freedom to all of us there. London had listened to our messages. At last, at last, here were all the weapons we needed, and explosives and grenades and mortars and ammunition. Now we could

do it, now we could fight. I remember you were delirious with joy, Christine, and I was as well. Auguste too. And it only got better. The parachutes opened, in their hundreds, and they were red, white and blue. Was there ever such a sight!

All we had to do now was to gather up what they had dropped for us and the fight could begin. Now we could take on anyone, anything they threw at us. For a moment I believed what we all wanted to believe, that the liberation had really begun. But as I was watching everyone rushing out to open the canisters and collect the weapons, all my excitement suddenly vanished, and a grim reality kicked in.

What were we thinking? A drop like this, on this scale, in broad daylight from this armada of planes must be madness. Did we really imagine the Germans were blind? They had eyes everywhere. You and I both knew that speed was now the only hope. We had to organise the collection of weapons, and prepare for the attack that would surely come, and soon.

When we heard the planes coming in again, most of us thought it was the Americans, with more weapons. Everyone was waving and cheering. But it wasn't the Americans, was it, Christine? We saw the black crosses on their wings.

They caught us out in the open collecting everything that had been dropped over the plateau. They strafed us, they bombed us, they blasted the villages in the Vercors to ruins.

The gliders came in, full of paratroopers, the tanks came up the passes, and all we had were rifles and a few Sten guns – nothing but pea shooters against their tanks, against their fighter planes.

Ten thousand of them were soon swarming all over the Vercors, hunting us down. Some villagers hid in the caves in the hills: the wounded, the women and children, the old people, everyone who could not run – they thought they would be safe. But there was no hiding place. The soldiers slaughtered whoever they found, murdered them.

You made us leave, Christine, and you were right. 'Live to fight another day,' you said. 'We could stay and die,

but I prefer to live,' you said. You saved my life. It wasn't the first time, and as it turned out, it wouldn't be the last. We clambered down ravines, through the forests, the gunfire and the screams echoing behind us.

And you, Auguste and I, we just kept walking, for twenty-four hours we kept walking, stopping only to drink in the streams, and to hold and comfort one another. Again and again you told us we should not blame ourselves, Christine, that what we had just witnessed was not our fault, but was a tragedy of war. That our day would come, freedom would come. For the first time on the trek down from the Vercors with you, I came so close to not believing that. But you picked me up, spurred me on.

We regrouped, gathered together all those who had survived, recruited at least as many again to replace those who had died. Auguste radioed for more supplies – and after the disaster on the Vercors they realised at last the urgency of our needs. And you spread the word far and wide amongst the Resistance groups and the Maquis in

France, and amongst the partisans over the border in Italy, so that the next time we rose up, when the Americans landed – and it would not be long – we should be ready, that we would not fail again.

What was it you used to say, Christine? 'France will be France again. Poland will be Poland.' You never doubted we would win, not for one moment, did you? You didn't let me doubt it, nor Auguste, nor anyone else either.

You were not there when I got careless, Christine, when I got caught. Just as well you weren't, when I come to think about it. But then maybe if you had been there, it would never have happened. You were up the mountains with Paul, our dear Paul Héraud – maybe the greatest man in my life – both of you making an army out of freedom fighters, Socialists, Communists, Gaullists, sorting out their squabbles, gathering them into one army of Resistance to fight the common enemy.

ALMOST THE END

Paul? Dumont might have been your code name – and like me you insisted we all used only our code names – but I never liked it. It never suited you. You were always Paul to me, even then, in my head. Paul Héraud, dear friend, freedom fighter supreme. And you are Paul to me now.

You hear that owl? You remember hearing one like that with me? We were waiting out on the hillside for a plane to come in, – Christine, Auguste, you, me – for yet another drop, and you tapped me on the shoulder and told me to listen. I thought you had heard the plane – but no, it was an owl. Like this one.

You seemed immortal to me at the time, Paul, to us all. With you there, we all knew we could win. You should never have been on that road at all. You were on your way on your motorbike to rescue a friend who had been arrested, when you drove into that German convoy, and they stopped you. You made a run for it, and they shot you down in the woods. We should have been with you – Christine, Auguste, me, all of us, one of us. You died alone, and the thought of that still troubles me, even now.

I've been to the place, Paul. A river running by, a wood filled with birdsong. If you had to die, countryman that you were, there was nowhere better, nowhere more peaceful. Auguste, Christine and me, we tried to carry the torch as

best we could, Paul, tried to keep the flame burning. But it never burnt so brightly after you were gone.

I wish you had been at my side today, Paul. You would have loved to see those children, living their lives in a free France, your beloved France that, more than anyone I know, you helped to make free. I felt that sometimes you were here today. I have often felt you watching over me, through the worst and best of times.

I am a grown man of ninety now, you hear me, Paul? Ninety! And you are still like a boyhood hero to me. I talk of you often, because I want people to hear about you. So few know of you. You lived quietly, a carpenter. You did what you did leading the Resistance, quietly. And you died, quietly.

✻ ✻ ✻

Strange, but I so nearly died the same way you did. We were in a car, came round a corner, and there they were,

German soldiers at a checkpoint. There were four of us, all agents: me, Christian Sorenson, Xan Fielding, and Claude Renoir, who was driving. You remember them, Paul? We were all in Claude's car, off to meet up with Resistance groups. We had plans to make, money to pass on to them, for food and supplies and the like. I gave them each an envelope full of banknotes, to spread it about a bit, to make it look less suspicious if any of us was searched. Just a regular trip, we thought. Everything was in order, papers, labour permits, everything. We had our story all prepared. If stopped, say we were strangers, that Sorenson and I had hitched a ride in Claude's car.

Anyway, we were on the edge of town, Digne it was, and there was the roadblock in front of us. I wasn't worried. We told our stories. They seemed satisfied, and waved us through. But then another car drew up. Milice. French Gestapo. I knew it at once. We told our story again: we were strangers hitching a ride. But this time we were searched, and they found the money. He was sharp-eyed this Milice officer, and noticed almost at once, from the numbers on the banknotes, that they came from the same batch. The numbers were sequential. We could not be strangers.

My fault. Very stupid, careless. We were taken to Digne prison where they slapped us about a bit, asked us questions we did not answer, and stood us facing a wall in the courtyard, hands above our heads. I thought they were going to shoot us there and then. Instead they threw us into a damp cell with a bucket in the corner and told us they would shoot us the next day.

When they came for us the next day it was to take us to Gestapo headquarters in the prison. We were interrogated there by a grey-haired man who looked like a bank manager. He had an unpleasant sidekick who was rather different – every inch a Nazi, blond hair, blue eyes, breeches, jackboots. They had no idea who we were and we didn't tell them. It would hardly have made things better for us if we had. Once they had finished with us they took us down to the death cell, as they called it, and left us there.

I sat there, angry at myself for my stupidity, and making my peace with Papa, Mama, Pieter, all the family at home. With everyone – and you too, Paul. Saying my goodbyes,

I suppose. It kept my mind off what was to come. I was wishing I had made a run for it and been shot down as you were, Paul. It would have been over quicker. To sit there in the darkness, waiting for it, was no way to spend my last night on this earth. We all knew it was simply a question now of how much we would be beaten up, and when we would be shot. Dawn was usual.

You loved Christine as much as I did, Paul. I know that well enough. We both knew she was fearless. But you did

not realise any more than I did then just how far she would go to save those she loved. You heard her singing that song often enough: 'Frankie and Johnny'. It became her song, our song. So we were sitting there in our death cell, waiting for the firing squad, for the sound of jackboots in the passageway outside. And we heard someone singing it. I thought I must be dreaming. No dream. It was Christine, in the street outside, singing to me, trying to find me – I knew that at once. So I joined in and sang along with her.

Do you remember how she hated cycling? She was as brave as a lion, but a ride on a bicycle terrified her. But she had cycled twenty kilometres to Digne to find me. She had heard we had been arrested, knew we were in Digne, in the Gestapo headquarters, but was not sure whether or not we had already been shot. So she sang her song outside in the street. Crazy, crazy woman! Wonderful woman.

And she got more wonderful, Paul. Once she heard me echoing our song, she marched straight into the prison

and demanded to speak to the officer in charge – Schenk he was called, the one who looked like a bank manager. How I would love to have been there to see it! I have so often tried to imagine it. She was far too modest ever to talk of it much afterwards.

What we do know is that she stood there looking him in the eye, and she must have said something like, 'I am a British agent, Pauline, Field Marshal Montgomery's niece. You are holding my husband here, Roger, with his friends, also British agents all of them, working with the Resistance. I am here to tell you that if you shoot them, as I am sure you intend to do, I will ensure that the Americans, who have already landed and are just a few days away, will make it their absolute priority to track you down and execute you. Or maybe the Resistance will find you first, in which case they will very probably tear you limb from limb.'

Schenk, like all the Germans by now, was nervous, knew the war was lost, and was looking for a way of saving his skin. Christine knew that. She saw the fear in his face. He blanched, gaped at her, swallowed a great deal, and then agreed to do what she said, providing she paid him two million francs, and gave him the assurance he asked for that he would be protected and treated as a prisoner of war. Christine told him she would be back in forty-eight hours with the money, but that if Schenk went back on his word and executed us, he could be quite sure the Resistance would wreak the most terrible revenge on him and his friends. Satisfied she had terrified the life out of him, she left.

Of course, we knew nothing of any of this, Paul. The song had given us hope, but we had no idea how Christine could possibly get us out of that place without a frontal attack, in which many would be bound to die, and which was very likely to fail anyway. After two days we had just about given up hope. When the Gestapo did come for us one morning, bound our wrists and marched us out, we were sure the end had come.

It was a strange walk, a kind of sleepwalk to death, out through the prison gates. I was not fearful, just sad I would not see Nan and the two girls again. Not see Christine again. We were marched towards the playing field where we knew people were taken to be shot.

But instead of being lined up for execution in the field, we were bundled into a black Citroën car. So it's to be another field, outside the town, I thought, and we'll be left in some ditch. They do that all the time. Schenk was there in the front seat in his uniform, beside the driver. We were driving fast, past saluting sentries, and out into the countryside.

Then we came round a bend, and there was Christine standing in the road. She didn't even look at us, but opened the front door of the car and squeezed in beside Schenk. The car drove on. No one spoke. I was still trying to work out what was going on. A few kilometres further on the car stopped.

Schenk got out and handed his revolver to Christine. I still could not work it out. You can't blame me, Paul, can you? This woman had achieved the impossible – broken us out of prison hours, minutes before we might have been executed, and spirited us away, not a shot fired.

Christine saw the bewilderment on my face. We hugged, we kissed, we laughed. Schenk stood there, forlorn and pathetic, our prisoner now.

That was another party you should have been there for, Paul, at Seigne it was, that evening. Christine there, Auguste there, everyone there. But not you. We drank to you, Paul, again and again that night, long into the night. We had escaped from inside the mouth of the wolf.

And you should have been there when the Resistance and the Americans liberated village after village, town after town. You should have seen the columns of dejected German prisoners, Charles de Gaulle striding down the Champs-Élysées in Paris, the joy in the streets. We were there, Pauline, Albert and Roger, the three musketeers, basking in the warmth of victory and our new-found freedom.

But it was not all joy, Paul. There was horrible retribution too. Collaborators were sought out, hunted down, treated shamefully.

Coming home after such a time was complicated. Nan and the girls were waiting for me, but I was not the same person who had left them. We had lived separate lives for too long. So much had happened to Nan, to me. It was as if my roots had to be regrafted. She did that for me. She wove a new life for us all, tended the family like a beloved garden, weeded it, looked after her flowers, loved them.

As soon as I could, I picked up where I had left off and I was back in the classroom, teaching, with forty fresh and expectant faces gazing up at me. The war had been an interruption. This was my real life: school, children. My nickname was 'Big Feet' again, and I heard behind me once more that same whispered 'Fee fi fo fum' as I left a classroom – so not everything had changed.

* * *

As for Christine, she had so much to offer, so much talent. But she had no country to go back to, no family,

no job. Poland had new occupiers now, from Soviet Russia. She was a troubled spirit, floundering in this strange new world of peace. She could not settle in post-war London. She went from job to job, her work in the Resistance unrecognised, her friends scattered. In the end, some wretched madman followed her home one day in London not long after the war, and murdered her. I was there at her funeral with some of those who had loved her.

A few years earlier, Nan and I had had another daughter. We called her Christine.

Two years later we had a boy, Nan and I, and we called him after you, Paul. He's a lovely boy, a good companion, and a fine man. You would like him.

It's been a long and fulfilling life, Paul, much of it spent in teaching and education, in England, Kenya, and Botswana, trying to give children the knowledge and understanding and love they need to make this a kinder, fairer, more peaceful world. You should have had such a life, Paul. The things you could have done. The times we would have had.

✳ ✳ ✳

That ruddy bell is clanging again. But I am ready for sleep now. Long life, long night. Be asleep soon. Won't hear it when it strikes again.

Look at that. There are flowers on my bedside table – red, white and almost-blue irises – the flowers that girl gave me at the party, the girl with the beautiful name, Jupjaapun Kaur. What did she say her name meant? Princess. That's it. Princess. I'm sure those flowers weren't there before. Maybe Kia brought them. Or maybe it was Niki, or Jay, or Paul. Dear Niki, dear Paul, dear Jay, dear Kia.

Sleep now.

Francis Cammaerts, 1916 – 2006,

died two weeks after

his 90th birthday party.

By Michael Morpurgo,

his nephew.

FRANCIS CAMMAERTS (1916-2006)

After graduating from Cambridge, Francis became a teacher. A fervent conscientious objector, he was sent to work on a farm in Lincolnshire. There he met and married Nancy Findlay. When his younger brother Pieter was killed in the RAF in 1941, aged 21, Francis decided he could no longer stay out of the war. He joined the Special Operations Executive as a secret agent, code name 'Roger', and set up a large network of loyal Resistance fighters across the south of France. He avoided capture until the last weeks of the war, when he was arrested at a roadblock. He was due to be shot, but was saved by his fellow SOE agent and friend, Christine Granville.

After the war Francis returned to teaching in the UK. He later founded the education department at the University of East Africa in Nairobi, and became principal of a new college of education in Botswana.

He retired to France with Nancy and his family, to the village of Le Pouget, in the Languedoc region of south west France.

NANCY (NAN) CAMMAERTS (NEE FINDLAY) (1917-2001)

Nan was born in Leeds and trained as a nurse. She met Francis on the farm where he lived and worked at the beginning of the war. They married in March 1941. Pieter, Francis's brother, was the best man at the wedding.

Nan was hugely supportive of Francis when he decided join up after Pieter's death. She was a strong woman with a sharp mind and great artistic flair, a much loved mother, grandmother and friend. She died in France in 2001.

PIETER CAMMAERTS (1919-1941)

Pieter trained as an actor at the Royal Academy of Dramatic Arts. Of his decision to enlist in the RAF, he said: 'Between you and me and the bed-post, I am scared stiff, but it is the best way of avoiding the tedious waiting in muddy trenches. The air is clean at least, and if the end comes it will be short and good.'

Pieter was a Sergeant Navigator – he wanted to be a pilot, but his eyesight was not good enough. His Bristol Blenheim bomber overshot the runway at RAF St Eval in Cornwall. Only one of the crew survived. Pieter is buried in Radlett, near his family home.

EMILE CAMMAERTS (PAPA) (1878-1953)

Born in Belgium, Emile was a freethinker and a poet. He moved to England with his wife, Tita Brema, a British actress. When the First World War broke out and German armies occupied Belgium, he wrote patriotic poems, *Carillion* and *Le Drapeau Belge* amongst them, and helped to organise a fund for Belgian war orphans.

After the war he became an art critic and academic, and converted to Christianity. He became a lay preacher in Radlett and was Professor of Belgian Studies at London University. He had six children, four girls – Marie, Elizabeth, Catherine, Jeanne – and two boys – Francis and Pieter.

HARRY RÉE (1914-1991)

Harry was a language teacher. He volunteered for the Special Operations Executive and, in 1943, he was parachuted into France and was active with the Resistance. After the war he returned to teaching and became the first Professor of Education at the University of York.

AUGUSTE FLOIRAS (1900-c.1995)

Code name 'Albert', Auguste was Francis Cammaert's radio operator in occupied France. He sent more clandestine messages out of France during the war than any other radio operator.

Earlier in the Occupation, his wife and daughter had been arrested and taken to Ravensbruck concentration camp. Francis went to Ravensbruck with Auguste after the war and found both of them still alive. Francis said of Auguste: 'You don't talk about a great friendship. It just is.'

PAUL HÉRAUD (1906-1944)

The last of five children, Paul was a carpenter, a great alpine climber and became a sergeant in the reserve.

When Germany occupied France in 1940, he created a formidable Resistance movement in the south of France.

In August 1944 he was stopped by German soldiers and shot while making his escape. Francis Cammaerts called him 'the most important man I've ever known'.

CHRISTINE GRANVILLE (1908-1952)

Maria Krystyna Janina Skarbek was born in Warsaw, the daughter of a wealthy Jewish family.

She escaped from occupied Poland at the outbreak of war, and offered her services in the struggle against Nazi Germany. Christine, now code name 'Pauline', was parachuted into the south of France in July 1944 and became part of the 'Jockey' Resistance network, commanded by Francis Cammaerts. She was brave, charismatic and persuasive, as her daring rescue of Francis from the firing squad shows.

Not long after the war, she died tragically, murdered in the lobby of a London hotel. Francis, amongst other friends, was at her funeral in London.

AUTHOR'S NOTE

Ray Jenkins's biography of Francis Cammaerts, *A Pacifist at War*, and Clare Mulley's *The Spy who Loved*, have both been immensely helpful to me in writing this book.

But it is the family, and especially Joanna (Jay) Cammaerts and Wole Wey, who have supported and guided my hand during the making of this story. I could not have done it, and would not have done it, without their kindness and support.

To have worked on this story with one of the great French illustrators, Barroux, was an honour and of course so appropriate. It was he who in large part inspired me to write it.

My thanks to Ali Dougal and Liz Bankes, my editors at Egmont, and to Laura Bird, who has art directed this book; Clare Morpurgo, my mentor in so much; Cally Poplak, my publisher at Egmont, also Ros Morpurgo and Vicki Berwick who helped prepare the script for me.

Michael Morpurgo

ILLUSTRATOR'S NOTE

Thank you to Michael for trusting me.

Thank you to Joanna for welcoming me into the heart of Le Pouget.

Using my own weapons, line and light, I have followed in Francis's footsteps to try to get closer to the man he was.

It has been a beautiful journey.

BARROUX

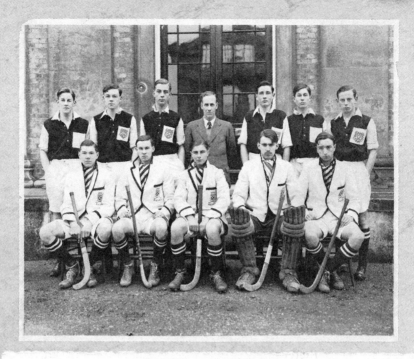

Francis (back row, third from the left) on the school hockey team

Emile and Tita Cammaerts
with four of their six children

Nancy Findlay as a young girl

Pieter

Snapshots of Francis

Francis (second row, sixth from the left) when he was a teacher

Francis in his military uniform

Nan Cammaerts, south of France 1947, with daughter Jay and friend

Francis and Auguste Floiras

Christine Granville in Palestine

Harry Rée

Christine Granville in 1942

Paul Héraud

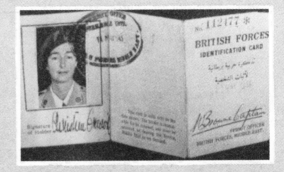

Christine's British Forces Identity Card

Francis and Nan